To Christo

The Rescue on the River

George Skinder

The Adventures of Freddie, the Little Fire Dragon

by George Skudera

The Avalanche At Snowville
The Rescue On The River
The Watch That Saved The Briar Woods Dam

(coming soon)

The Ring Of Fire
The Surprise In The Mailbox
The Briar Woods Sluggers

Follow Your Dreams

HARMON

SNO

EVERGREEN

BR

REDWOOD
FOREST

UNEXPLORED

SUNNY

DESERT

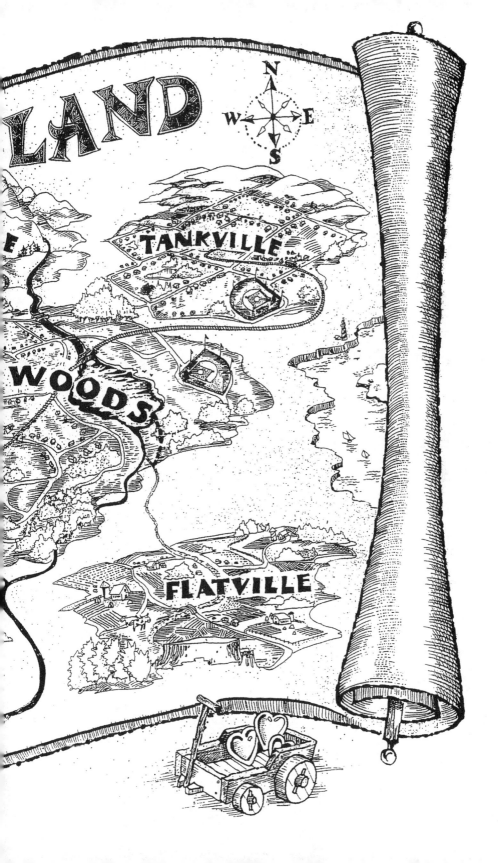

The Adventures of *Freddie the little Fire Dragon*

The Rescue on the River

by *George Skudera*

First published by AuthorHouse 10/18/05

ISBN: 1-4208-1691-8 (sc)

Library of Congress Control Number: 2004099402

Printed in the United States of America

This book is printed on acid-free paper.

The Adventures of Freddie, the Little Fire Dragon, logos and characters are trademarks of George Skudera

The Rescue on the River

Freddie was gently awakened by the sounds of chirping birds in the branches of the tree outside his window. He climbed out of bed, and hopped over to the open window, and looked out. He looked first to the left; then to the right, and then upwards at the pretty blue sky.

Freddie turned away from the window, and hopped back to his bed. He brought his head down to the floor, so he could look under it.

With a big smile on his face, he whispered, "Tanga. The sun is shining. It's going to be a nice day. The rain clouds are all gone. I have an idea as to what we can do today!"

1

Tanga began to crawl out from under the bed. He looked at Freddie, and rubbing his eyes said, "I can't believe it is morning already. Freddie, the sun is really, really bright."

Tanga stopped talking for a moment, to yawn.

"Freddie, did you say you have an idea? Does it have anything to do with going outside and playing?"

"Yes, Tanga. Do you want to hear about it?"

Tanga answered, "Sure! I can't wait to go outside. All we were doing for the past two days while it was raining was watching television and playing Rainy Day kinds of games."

"Are you ready?"

"Yes Freddie. Tell me! Tell me!"

Freddie began. "Well, I am going to ask my mother if she would pack a picnic lunch and take us to the park, by the river, to play."

Tanga began hopping up and down, yelling "Goodie, Goodie. I want to go down the slide that goes through the big hole in the Frakus tree."

Freddie replied, "It's going to be a race who goes down the slide first. That's my favorite ride in the whole playground."

"Freddie, rather than race to see who goes first, why don't we go down it together. I can sit behind you and hug you tight. You know, it's a little scary!"

"Tanga, It's not scary for me. Nothing is scary for me! I'm a fire dragon; even if I am only a pre-school fire dragon, at that."

As Freddie started to make his bed, he began wondering if his idea would really come true. He turned around, and looking at Tanga said, "Let me see. What day is it? Tuesday? Wednesday? My mother always goes shopping on ...Tuesday."

Tanga replied, "You are asking the wrong one. All I know is that it is a beautiful, sunny day and we are going to go play outside."

Freddie hopped over to his bedroom closet door and opened it. On the back of the door hung a big calendar. He looked at the numbers that were crossed out ... 1,2,3,4,5, and then the days of the week.

Freddie put his fingers to his lips, thinking. He turned to look at Tanga. "I don't remember if I crossed out yesterday. Today is either Tuesday or Wednesday."

Tanga said, "Make a wish Freddie. Oh, please let it be Wednesday!"

Freddie hopped over to the open window, and looking out said, "I wish, I wish, I wish, I wish a million wishes that today is Wednesday!"

Freddie had just finished making his wish, when he heard his mother calling, "Freddie, wake up. It is time for breakfast. Wake up Tanga."

In a matter of seconds, Freddie and Tanga came hopping into the kitchen. As soon as Freddie had climbed onto his chair, he called out "Mommy. Is it Tuesday or Wednesday today?"

Both Freddie and Tanga had their fingers crossed under the table, hoping that the answer would be Wednesday.

Freddie's mother said, "Wednesday."

Freddie startled his mother, when he yelled out, "OK! OK! My wish came true!"

About the same time he was yelling out "OK", he felt something hitting his tail. He bent backwards, and after looking down at the floor under the table, began laughing out loud.

Freddie's mother said, "Freddie, what is so funny?"

"It's Tanga. He is wagging his tail and it is hitting **my** tail."

"Now, Freddie. What is so very special about today being Wednesday?"

"Well, because it rained for the past two days and I made a wish that we could all go on a picnic to the park with the playground by the river. "

Freddie's mother looked at him, her eyes saddened, before saying, "Freddie, I would love to, but ..."

Before Freddie's mother could finish her sentence, Freddie's big blue eyes began to fill up with tears.

Freddie's mother, seeing tears beginning to trickle from Freddie's eyes, continued her sentence " ... I usually go shopping on Tuesdays, but because it had rained for the past two days, I was planning to go today, Wednesday."

Tanga leaned over and hugged Freddie, his eyes filling up with tears.

Freddie's mother looked down at them and began to get tears in her eyes.

The next words that Freddie and Tanga would hear were, "Let's go on a picnic today at the park, by the river. I'm going to do my shopping tomorrow, Thursday."

Freddie and Tanga climbed out of their chairs and began hopping up and down, again and again, causing the dishes on the kitchen counter to rattle.

Freddie's mother called out, "You will have to stop hopping. I don't want to spend the day in the kitchen cleaning up a bunch of broken dishes. Freddie, go to your room and pack up a few toys that you want to take to the park."

Freddie hopped straight to his room, with Tanga close behind. He took the big towel lying on the floor from last night's bath, and began to put some of his favorite Dragon Action Figures on it.

While he was doing that, Tanga hopped over to the far corner of the bedroom, and picked up his pink ball. He tossed it on the towel that

Freddie was busy tugging on the ends of to make a sack.

Freddie had just begun to tie a knot into the towel that was stuffed with his toys and Tanga's pink ball, when his mother called out, "Are you ready yet? I have the wagon hitched and a picnic basket filled with sandwiches, and your favorite snacks."

"I just have to finish tying the knot in my sack that I filled with Tanga's ball and my toys."

A minute later, Freddie and Tanga were in the kitchen looking for the handle of the kitchen broom that had come loose and fallen off the day before. If he were lucky, the broom would still be in two pieces: the handle and the straw bottom.

Luck was with Freddie. In the corner of the kitchen, standing against the wall was the broom: both pieces. He grabbed the handle and pushed it through the knot in his sack. Then he lifted it up, resting the broom handle on his tiny shoulder.

Freddie, turned to Tanga and said, "Let's move out! Playtime is soon to begin!"

After Freddie and Tanga were in the wagon seat, and securely buckled, Freddie's mother slipped into the wagon harness, and with a single tug, started the wagon rolling out on to the deep-rutted, gravel road.

During the journey to the park Freddie was telling Tanga jokes he had heard on Giggle Toons the day before: the day that it rained, and rained, and rained.

It wasn't long before Tanga recognized the entrance to the park and started pulling on Freddie, pointing in the direction of the playground.

Freddie turned in the direction Tanga was pointing to and yelled out, "There's the giant Frakus tree."

Standing tall, and reaching high above all the other trees in the park, was the tallest branch, the very top of the Frakus tree.

Tanga said to Freddie, "I hope the slide is still there!"

Freddie replied, "It's there. We'll be sliding down it in a couple of minutes."

He called to his mother, "How much longer Mommy?"

"Just a few minutes more, Freddie."

Freddie and Tanga started giggling and laughing. The afternoon of fun was about to begin.

In a few minutes, just like Freddie's mother said, the wagon was parked under a giant tree. After the picnic basket was placed on top of the bright, blue blanket that rested on the soft grass, she hopped back to the wagon.

Freddie's mother began unfastening Freddie and Tanga's wagon seat belts, and then picking them up one at a time, placed them gently on the ground.

Freddie and Tanga were ready to run down the path to the playground, when Freddie's mother said, "Just a minute! We have rules that we will follow today. Let's see... First, there is to be no pushing and shoving. Second, when you hear me calling you, come back to the blanket as fast as you can. Double hop! Triple hop... if you can! Lastly, make sure you don't leave any of your toys at the playground when you come back to the blanket."

Freddie and Tanga, looking at Freddie's mother, stood at attention and saluted her, just like the soldiers they saw on Giggle Toons the day before. They turned toward the direction of the playground.

After Freddie yelled out, "Let's roll," they hopped down the path, taking single hops first and then double hops.

As they hopped along, Freddie's mother began thinking, "Freddie isn't going to be a pre-school fire dragon much longer. He is already doing double hops. He also gets a good puff of fire out, every once in a while, after he finishes eating his vegetables. I don't even know how much longer I will be able to lift him up into his wagon seat."

Freddie's mother watched Freddie and Tanga until they reached the playground. She could hear their yells and laughter as they climbed up the ladder to the slide that would take them down and through the giant Frakus tree.

She decided to prepare lunch from the food that was in the picnic basket. Freddie's mother knew from experience that when they would return to the blanket, after she called them for lunch, it would be the wrong time to just begin making sandwiches.

They would be hungry, and not wanting to waste any time waiting for lunch to be prepared. They would want to eat and hop back to the playground as fast as their little legs could take them.

Freddie's mother began to think to when she was a little pre-school fire dragon. Her mother took her to the same playground. She could remember her mother saying, "It's a fun day for you Betty, but a lot of work for your mother. But, it is certainly worth it."

While Freddie's mother didn't quite understand her mother's words then, she certainly understood them now, and appreciated what her mother had done for her, time and time again.

After Freddie's mother made lunch, she repacked the sandwiches and snacks into the picnic basket, and began reading the Briar Woods Herald, the daily newspaper that had all the gossip, and more importantly, all the coupons that she would tear out and bring to the supermarket tomorrow. The money she saved with coupons always seemed to cover Freddie's "Can I have this?" requests.

As she turned the pages of the newspaper, she felt her eyes getting heavy. She said to herself, "A five minute Dragon Nap would feel so very good, but, I can't. Freddie and Tanga are at the playground."

The harder she tried not to fall asleep, the heavier her eyelids seemed to get. She put down the newspaper on the bright blue blanket, and after listening to the voices and laughter of Freddie and Tanga in the distance, and knowing that they were safe, fell asleep.

Freddie and Tanga eventually got tired of riding the slide through the giant Frakus tree.

Freddie looked at Tanga and said, "What do you want to do next?"

Tanga replied, "Play ball!"

Freddie untied the sack, and after taking out Tanga's pink ball, tied the sack up with a tight knot, and slid the broom handle through it.

Tanga yelled out, "Let me kick first!"

"OK."

Freddie and Tanga played ball, kicking it back and forth to each other, over and over again. It wasn't until they decided that they would go back to the bright, blue blanket and have some Goo Goo cookies and Fire Juice, that Tanga said " I bet I can kick the ball farther than you!"

Freddie said, "No way. I'm a pre-school fire dragon. I can kick the ball out of the playground!"

Tanga laughed, saying, "I bet you a Dragon Pop you can't! If you were a grownup fire dragon; maybe."

Freddie was anxious to take Tanga's bet. He said, "Give me the ball Tanga. I can do it!"

Tanga handed Freddie the ball saying, "Where do you want me to stand to catch it?

Freddie pointed saying, "Go all the way back, to the edge of the hill that leads down to the river."

Moments after Tanga hopped to the spot that Freddie pointed to, Freddie called out, "Get ready!"

Freddie put the pink ball on the ground. He began hopping backwards. After ten hops he stopped.

He stared at the ball for a few seconds before he looked up and yelled, "Here it comes!"

Freddie started hopping toward Tanga's pink ball. He started with a single hop, then a double, and then for the first time in his life, Freddie did a triple hop!

His right foot landed right up against the ball, sending it flying up in the air, almost as high as the very top branch of the Frakus tree.

Both Freddie and Tanga stood in amazement as they watched the pink ball fly across the playground.

Tanga yelled to Freddie, "My ball! It's going to roll down the hill towards the river!"

Freddie was just about ready to start hopping towards Tanga, when he remembered his mother's rules that were to be obeyed at the park. "No pushing and shoving. When you hear me calling you, come back to the blanket as fast as you can. Double hop! Triple hop if you can! Lastly, make sure you don't leave any of your toys at the playground when you come back to the blanket."

Freddie turned around, and hopped over to where he had left his sack of toys. He grabbed the broom handle, and swung it up onto his tiny shoulder. He spun around and started hopping towards Tanga.

By the time Freddie reached Tanga, the ball had rolled down the hill and out of sight.

Tanga started crying. "Freddie, we have to get my ball. It's very special to me. It's the one that was given to me by the owner of the pet shop, the day you took me to your house to live.

Freddie said, "No problem! I know we are not supposed to leave the playground, but we really aren't. There is no fence dividing the playground from the steep hill."

Tanga looked at Freddie, wiping the tears from his eyes. "You are right Freddie, it is kind of a part of the playground. It should only take a minute or two to go down the hill, get my pink ball, and hop up to this very spot we are standing on."

Freddie, looking at Tanga said, "Let's roll!"

Tanga grabbed Freddie's hand. Together they started down the hill. They had only made two hops when Tanga slipped on some wet grass and fell to the ground, taking Freddie, and his sack of toys with him.

Freddie yelled out, "We're going down!"

Down the hill they tumbled. It seemed like forever that they were tumbling.

When they stopped, they stood up, only to find out that they were only a few feet from the edge of the river. Floating in front of them was a tiny log raft that was tied to a stake in the ground at the water's edge.

As they were brushing the dirt off of themselves, Tanga yelled out, "My pink ball. It's on the raft! Look!"

A moment later, Tanga yelled to Freddie, "Your sack of toys and the broom handle are on the raft also. It's next to my ball! We are both lucky!"

Freddie said, "Great. I was wishing, wishing, a million wishes, that your ball didn't roll into the river. If it did, it would have been lost, lost forever. I forgot all about my sack of toys and the broom handle in all the excitement."

Tanga said, "I'll go out on the raft and get my ball and your sack of toys."

Freddie replied, "No. We will both go out on the raft. You can't hold your ball and put my sack on your shoulder by yourself. Plus, I think that my sack of toys is too heavy for you to pick up."

Tanga said, "We better do it now. I think it is almost lunchtime, and your mother will be calling us to eat! If we don't answer, she will hop over to the playground. If we don't make it back up to the top of the hill in time we will be in big trouble!"

Freddie replied, "You're right. Big trouble!"

Freddie and Tanga hopped over to the edge of the riverbank, and at Freddie's command, "Hop", hopped from the grassy riverbank onto the raft.

The raft started to rock back and forth, causing Freddie and Tanga to fall onto the deck of the raft.

It wasn't until after they got back on their feet and hopped over to the pink ball, that Freddie yelled out, "Tanga, the stick that was holding the rope that was holding the raft against the river bank, pulled out of the ground! We are drifting away! We are drifting down the river!"

Tanga started crying.

Freddie said, "Don't cry Tanga. Yell for help!"

Together they began yelling for help, but the steep hill that bordered the river was so high, their voices could not be heard. They yelled for help over and over again, as the tiny raft continued to drift, farther and farther down the river.

Meanwhile, up the river, across the playground, and down the path that led to the bright blue blanket, Freddie's mother was busy setting the lunch plates and napkins for Freddie and Tanga's lunch.

After taking the sandwiches and Fire Juice cups from the picnic basket, and placing them next to the paper plates, she turned towards the playground and called, "Freddie! Tanga! Lunch time!"

She waited for a reply. There was none.

Freddie's mother began hopping down the path to the playground, unaware that anything was wrong. As she got closer and closer to the playground she called out, "Freddie! Tanga! Lunch time!"

Still there was no answer.

When she reached the Fracus tree and saw no sign of Freddie and Tanga, she began to panic.

"Freddie! Tanga! Where are you?"

At first, she thought they might have been playing hide-and-seek with her. Perhaps they would hop out from behind a berry bush and yell, "Surprise!"

Hearing no answer from either Freddie or Tanga, she yelled out, " Freddie and Tanga. This is no time to play games. Come out wherever you are!"

Still there was no answer.

She hopped down to the other end of the playground where two young fire dragons were flying their kites.

"Did you see a little pre-school fire dragon and his pet, a little druff, playing here?"

"No. We just came here a few minutes ago."

Freddie's mother decided to hop as quickly as she could, in triple hops, to the little hut where the playground attendant stayed, which was at the opposite side of the playground. Tears began rolling down her eyes. She began sobbing.

As she approached the hut, she began yelling, "My little boy, and his pet druff are missing."

The attendant came out of his hut and put his arm on her shoulder saying, "Please calm down. They are probably playing in the Oooz

Puddles behind the berry bushes. I had the same incident happen twice last week. Come with me."

Together then began hopping toward the Oooz Puddles.

Meanwhile, the little raft that Freddie and Tanga were stranded on, continued to drift further and further down the river.

Freddie said, "I wish I knew how to swim."

Tanga replied, "Me too."

As the tiny raft began to approach a heavy wooded area, there were large trees with branches that stretched across the width of the river. Freddie began to hear familiar sounds.

He turned to Tanga and said, "Do you hear those sounds?"

Tanga turned his head in the direction that Freddie was looking, and listened. "What sounds Freddie? Fire dragon sounds? Maybe we are going to be rescued!"

"No, Tanga. The sounds I think I am hearing are the sounds of giant buzzards. My mother told me that they are always out hunting for food. Any kind of food!"

Tanga looked at Freddie, his eyes and mouth open wide, "Any kind of food? Like us?"

"I don't know Tanga. Maybe."

As the tiny raft drifted under the cover of the giant tree branches, Freddie heard a splash in the water to his left. He turned toward the sound of the splash. Chills began running up and down his back. "Did you hear that Tanga?"

"Yes. I'm scared! Could it be an alligator coming over to eat us?"

"I can't see it clearly. I just see splashing!"

As the raft drifted closer to the object in the water, Freddie pulled the broom handle loose from his sack of toys saying, "Tanga, if it is an alligator, I'll scare it away with my sword."

Tanga replied, "Freddie, this is no time to play! You have a wooden broom handle in your hand, not a sword. You are not going to scare anything away with that!"

As they approached the object, Freddie and Tanga were so frightened, that they each could hear the sounds of their hearts beating.

Suddenly, Freddie said, "Tanga, what is in the water is not an alligator, but a little baby buzzard. It must have fallen out of its nest. We have to rescue it before it drowns."

Tanga yelled out, "Not before it drowns, but before the alligator that is coming across the river, and from behind the baby buzzard, eats it for lunch!"

Freddie yelled out, "We have to save it!"

Tanga replied, "How!"

Freddie put his fingers to his lips for a moment, before yelling out, "I have a plan!"

Tanga yelled out, "A plan? What is it?"

Freddie handed Tanga the broom handle saying, "Hold this out to the baby buzzard when we get close enough."

Tanga grabbed it saying, "How are we going to get close enough. We are drifting, and the alligator will be next to the baby buzzard in a minute, or maybe less."

Freddie said, "Hang on! We are going for a ride!"

Freddie hopped to the very end of the tiny raft, and turned around putting his tail all the way into the water. He then began swishing it back and forth, like an oar in a rowboat. Slowly, the raft began to turn in the direction of the baby buzzard.

Tanga yelled, "It's working, Freddie, but the alligator is gaining on us! He is going to get to the baby buzzard and have his lunch, before we can get there. You have to swish your tail faster! Faster Freddie!"

Freddie swished his tail faster and faster. The tiny raft was gaining speed and the race to the baby buzzard was getting closer and closer.

Tanga kept yelling, "Faster Freddie! Faster!"

The raft was almost within range for Tanga to stick out the broom handle to the baby buzzard to grab onto, when the big alligator came up alongside the raft with his mouth wide open, ready to snap his jaws on the baby buzzard.

It was at that very moment that Tanga put the broom handle into the big alligator's mouth.

With one snap of the alligator's jaws, the long broom handle was reduced from a make-believe sword, to something the size of a Popsicle stick.

Tanga yelled, "It's too late. The alligator is going to eat the baby buzzard!"

Freddie yelled back to Tanga, "It's never too late! Stand back!"

Freddie took a deep breath, and facing the alligator, who now had his mouth wide open, and his rows of white teeth ready to snap down on the helpless, baby buzzard, spit out a stream of fire directly into the alligator's mouth.

The alligator spun around leaving a trail of steam coming out of his nostrils, and dove to the bottom of the river never to be seen again.

Freddie hopped to the back of the raft and after putting his tail as deep into the water as he could, began swishing it back and forth, harder and harder, until the raft got close enough for Tanga to reach out and grab the baby buzzard.

As soon as the baby buzzard was safely on the raft, Freddie yelled out, "Untie my sack and dump my action figures out of it. We need to wrap the baby buzzard in my towel. We have to dry its feathers so it doesn't catch a cold!"

Moments after Freddie gave Tanga his instructions, there was a big thud that rocked the raft, knocking Freddie and Tanga down.

When they turned to see what made the thud, they started yelling, "Don't eat us! Please don't eat us!"

Standing in front of Freddie and Tanga was a giant buzzard.

The buzzard looked first at Freddie and then at Tanga, before saying "I'm not going to harm you. I want to thank you for saving my baby who fell out of his nest. You are heroes!"

Freddie and Tanga looked at the giant buzzard and said at the same time, "I thought you were going to eat us for lunch."

"I'm afraid not. What I would like to do is reward you in some way for saving my baby."

Freddie looked up at the giant buzzard and said, "We don't want any reward. We did what had to be done to save your baby."

Freddie heard Tanga begin to cry.

When Freddie turned to look at Tanga, Tanga cried out, "Mrs. Buzzard, we are lost! We too need to be rescued! We need to get back to a playground far up the river. I'm sure that Freddie's mother is frightened just like you were, and crying like I am."

The giant buzzard stood silent for a minute or two before saying, "I have a plan. But first, let me put my baby back in his nest, and give him something to eat."

The giant buzzard unwrapped Freddie's towel from the baby buzzard and handed it to Freddie. "Here, why don't you wrap your toys in the towel before they roll off of the raft and into the water."

As Freddie grabbed the towel, the giant buzzard grabbed her baby, and flew up into the air, and in the direction of the giant trees with the branches that stretched from one side of the river to the other.

It was only a few minutes after Freddie had neatly packed his toys into the towel and finished tying a single knot, that Freddie and Tanga felt a heavy thud on the opposite end of the raft that they were sitting on.

Tanga yelled, "It's Mrs. Buzzard."

The giant buzzard looked at Freddie and Tanga and said, " Now it is *my* time to play hero."

The giant buzzard began pulling on the rope tied to the tiny raft, which was floating in the water.

When the end of the rope came out of the water and rested on the raft, Freddie said, "The stick is still attached to it. Mrs. Buzzard, that is the stick that was stuck into the ground to hold the raft at the bank of the river. It was right by the spot we landed, after rolling down the hill by the playground."

Tanga yelled out, "Can you take us there?"

"I'll try my hardest!"

After getting the end of the rope tightly clenched in her feet, the giant buzzard flapped her wings, and lifted upwards.

Once the rope became taught, she turned in the direction of where the raft had drifted from, and began pulling the raft with Freddie and Tanga upstream.

Freddie and Tanga began yelling, "Faster! Faster! We are going home!"

By the time the giant buzzard reached the spot where Freddie and Tanga had landed after rolling down the hill, she dropped to the ground.

With a single peck of her powerful beak, she made a deep hole into the ground by the riverbank, not far from the spot where the other hole was. She then grabbed the stick in her beak, and pushed it deep into the ground.

The giant buzzard turned to Freddie and Tanga saying, "You are home. It is safe to hop off of the raft."

As Freddie and Tanga were hopping off of the raft, Freddie said, "Mrs. Buzzard, you are a hero! How can we ever thank you for saving us. Can I give you a reward?"

The giant buzzard smiled, " I don't want any reward. I only did what was necessary to save you and Tanga."

Freddie said, "Thank you Mrs. Buzzard for saving us and not eating us."

The giant buzzard smiled and said, "I must leave now and take care of my babies."

Freddie and Tanga were watching the giant buzzard slowly disappear into the distance, when Freddie yelled out, "Tanga, Mrs. Buzzard is turning. She is coming back!"

"Freddie! Do you think she changed her mind about eating us?"

Freddie replied, "I don't think so. Let's wait for her right here."

The giant buzzard made a single circle over Freddie and Tanga before it dropped to the ground, only inches away from them.

Freddie and Tanga stood motionless. They were so frightened, that they each could hear the sound of their hearts beating.

The giant buzzard stood motionless for a few seconds, staring first at Freddie, and then Tanga, before saying, "Don't be frightened. I didn't come back to eat you. There is something I would like to give you. I will be back in one minute."

The giant buzzard flapped her wings and headed up into the tall trees on top of the hill.

Freddie said, "Tanga, What could Mrs. Buzzard have forgotten to give us?"

"Freddie, I'm still a little scared."

No sooner had Tanga finished speaking, when the giant buzzard returned, and landed a few feet from Freddie and Tanga, holding a tree branch in her beak.

She looked at Freddie and said, "I took this from the tallest and the strongest, tree on top of the hill, the Frakus tree. Put it through the knot on your sack so you can carry it over your shoulder, while you climb up the hill.

Freddie, some day when you are all grown up, I am certain that you will be the tallest, the bravest, and the strongest fire dragon in all of Briar Woods. I must go now."

As the giant buzzard flapped her wings and soared up into the air, Freddie and Tanga waved goodbye. They didn't stop waving until the giant buzzard disappeared from view.

Tanga turned to Freddie and said, "Let's move out!"

As they reached the top of the hill, Freddie carrying his sack of toys and Tanga his pink ball, they were greeted by lots of fire dragons, and most important of all, Freddie's mother.

Freddie's mother hugged him and Tanga. "We all thought you were lost. Some of us were afraid that the giant buzzard that was flying over the playground near the Frakus tree a little while ago had taken you."

Holding back her tears, she said, "I'm so happy you are safe."

Freddie looked up at his mother, and said "We're OK. Is it time for lunch?"

They were all laughing as they headed down the path to the bright, blue blanket and the picnic basket that had Freddie's favorite sandwiches, snacks, and drink; Fire Juice.

The journey back was accompanied with the cheers from all the fire dragons that had formed the search party for them.

As they were eating lunch, Freddie's mother said, "Do you want to tell me where you were, and what happened today?"

Freddie looked at his mother and said, "If I tell you my story, will you tell me one?"

Freddie's mother hugged him, and after giving him a big kiss said, "Yes."

As Freddie began to tell the story to his mother, Tanga slid over to him and hugged his leg. Tanga looked at Freddie's mother and said, "You are not going to believe it."

Freddie's mother turned to Tanga, and said, "You are not going to believe the story I'm going to tell you."

They all broke out in laughter.

It wasn't until the next morning, that Freddie's mother would find the branch of the Frakus tree standing against the wall in the corner of the kitchen, next to the straw bottom of the broom.

After picking it up in her hand, she hopped over to the living room where Freddie was watching television with Tanga, and said "Freddie, where did this come from? Where is the real broom handle that you put through the knot in your sack, that you took to the park?"

Freddie hesitated for a moment before saying, "Oh, that's part of the story I forgot to tell you about yesterday."

Freddie's mother said, "Do you want to tell me about it now?"

"No, Mommy. Let's keep it a secret!"

"Freddie, maybe you could tell me your secret when we have our Goo Goo cookies and milk after we come back from the supermarket."

Freddie looked up at his mother and said, "OK."

Freddie's mother looked down at him with tears in her eyes and said "Freddie, you are going to grow up to be the biggest, bravest, and strongest fire dragon in all of Briar Woods."

With that, she bent over, and after kissing him said, "I love you."

Freddie looked up at his mother with tears in his big blue eyes and answered, "I love you too, Mommy.

The End

Hi Boys and Girls,

I hope you enjoyed reading one of the first books, in the series of The Adventures of Freddie, the little Fire Dragon titled:

The Rescue On The River

Other books in Part 1 of the series:

The Avalanche At Snowville
The Watch That Saved The Briar Woods Dam
The Ring Of Fire
The Surprise In The Mailbox
The Briar Woods Sluggers

Interested in joining Freddie's Fan Club? Send your name and address to:

> Freddie
> P.O. Box 194
> Farmingdale, NJ 07727
> USA

P.S.   Let me know what you liked best about the story.

Freddie

The Adventures
of *Freddie* the little
Fire Dragon

The
Avalanche at Snowville

by
George Skudera

The Adventures of Freddie the little Fire Dragon

The Watch that Saved the Briar Woods Dam

by George Skudera

The Adventures of Freddie the little Fire Dragon

The Ring of Fire

by George Skudera

The Adventures
of *Freddie* the little
Fire Dragon

The Surprise in the Mailbox

by George Skudera

The Adventures of *Freddie* the little Fire Dragon

The Briar Woods Sluggers

by George Skudera

About the author

The author's passion to preserve the innocence of youth has resulted in the creation of a series of children's stories that take place in a land absent of crime and violence. His series, *The Adventures of Freddie, the Little Fire Dragon*, focus on family values, friendship, caring and sharing with others.

George Skudera has uniquely combined everyday life events and happenings with his whimsical imagination, resulting in stories that are filled with warmth and vitality and certain to capture the minds and hearts of its readers, both young and old.

His ability to bring life to his make believe characters will have you wanting to cheer for their accomplishments, laugh out loud from the humor each adventure contains, and bring a tear or two to your eyes from the deep emotions that are unleashed between the main characters; Freddie, his mother, and his pet Tanga.

Sketch Page

Notes